YAWN!

For Kathy—I can always count on you!
—T.S.

To Byron, who jumps over fences in style.
I mean, *stile*.
—T.C.

The illustrations in this book were created digitally.

Library of Congress Control Number 2020949945
ISBN 978-1-4197-4630-7

Text © 2021 Tammi Sauer
Illustrations © 2021 Troy Cummings
Book design by Hana Anouk Nakamura
Cover © 2021 Abrams Appleseed

Printed and bound in China
10 9 8 7 6 5 4 3 2 1

For bulk discount inquiries, contact specialsales@abramsbooks.com.

ABRAMS The Art of Books
195 Broadway, New York, NY 10007
abramsbooks.com

ONE SHEEP, TWO SHEEP

PLACES, EVERYONE!

by **Tammi Sauer**

illustrated by **Troy Cummings**

Abrams Appleseed
New York

Good night, my wonderful farm friends.
It's time for sleep.

I must
count sheep.

One sheep.

Two sheep.

Three sheep.

Whoa! Whoa! Whoa! **A CHICKEN?!**
I'm sorry, but this is serious bedtime business.
I count **SHEEP**, okay? Just sheep!

Four sheep.
Five sheep.
Six sheep.

EEP!

Oh, for crowing out loud!
Nice effort, Pig.
But I need to sleep.
Bring on the sheep.

Seven
sheep.

Eight
sheep.

Nine
sheep.

Cock-a-doodle-DO WE NEED TO REVIEW?

Counting **SHEEP** helps me sleep.

And you all don't look the slightest bit sheepish.

Now where was I?
Let's see . . .
One, two, three, four, five,
six, seven, eight, nine . . .

YAWWWWN

TEN sheep.

STOP!

I'm sorry to break the news,
but you are **NOT** sheep.

Hey, sheep! Come back!